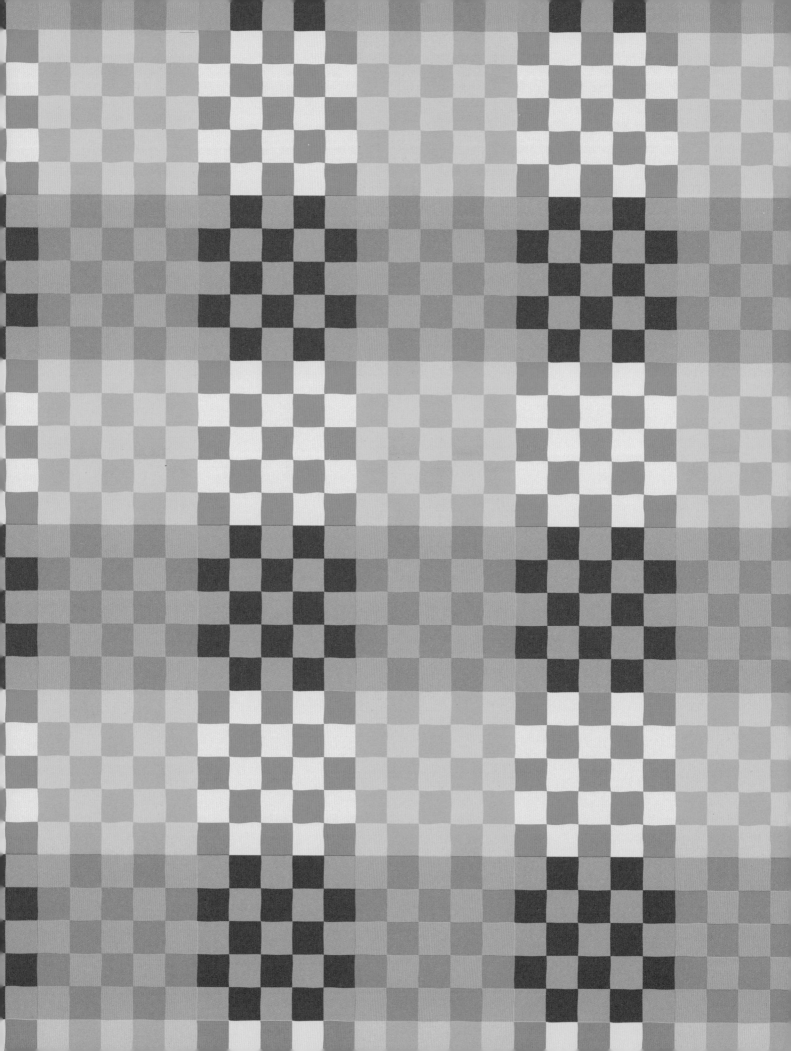

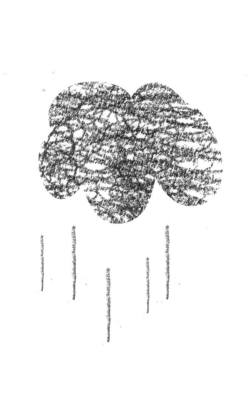

For Izzy, Flynn, Phoebe, Ruby,
Oscar, and Tennyson. With love xxx

Text copyright © 2023 by A. H. Benjamin
Illustrations copyright © 2023 by Laura Vitória Jäger

Published by Bushel & Peck Books, a family-run publishing house in
Fresno, California, that believes in uplifting children with the highest
standards of art, music, literature, and ideas. Find beautiful books for
gifted young minds at www.bushelandpeckbooks.com.

Type set in LTC Kennerley Pro, Aunt Mildred, and Calder

Bushel & Peck Books is dedicated to fighting illiteracy all over the
world. For every book we sell, we donate one to a child in need—
book for book. To nominate a school or organization to receive free
books, please visit www.bushelandpeckbooks.com.

LCCN: 2023941456
ISBN: 978-1-63819-135-3

First Edition

Printed in China

1 3 5 7 9 10 8 6 4 2

THE
Naughty Bench

ILLUSTRATED BY

A. H. BENJAMIN
LAURA VITÓRIA JÄGER

BUSHEL
& PECK
BOOKS

It was going to be a bad morning for Room 4. To begin with, the weather was horrendous. Then the class learned that the trip to the zoo that afternoon was cancelled. On top of that, Miss Cross, their teacher, had an awful headache.

"I'm not in a good mood!" she said.

Neither were the children. They sat miserably at their desks, their hair dripping wet, their noses red from the cold.

The trouble soon started.

Miss Cross was writing on the blackboard when someone blew a loud raspberry. *Thbbft!*

"Who did that?" she asked.

Everyone pointed to Flynn.

"Go and sit on the bench!" ordered Miss Cross.
So Flynn trotted off to the back of the room
and sat on a long, long bench.

Not long after, sisters Ruby and Phoebe started bickering.

"What's going on?" demanded Miss Cross.

"Ruby called me ugly!" whined Phoebe.

"She called me ugly first!" whined Ruby.

"For goodness sakes, you're twins!" Miss Cross cried. "You look *exactly* the same!"

But Ruby and Phoebe went on arguing.
"I'm not having that," said Miss Cross.
"Both of you, go and sit on the bench!"
   Scowling at each other, Ruby and
Phoebe did as they were told.

"Miss, may I go to the toilet?" asked Oscar.
"Yes," said Miss Cross. "Don't be long."
But Oscar was ages.
"Where is that boy?" wondered Miss Cross.
Then something that looked like a mummy from ancient Egypt shuffled into the classroom.

Some children screamed.

"What on Earth are you doing?" asked Miss Cross.

The mummy mumbled something that nobody could understand. And without being told, it tottered to the bench and sat down.

Miss Cross sighed. "My headache is getting worse!" she complained.

Outside, the weather was still bad. The rain lashed at the windows, and the wind whistled through the eaves.

Just then, Miss Cross was called to the office.
"I shan't be long!" she said as she rushed out.
As soon as Miss Cross was gone, Tennyson
started lobbing paper balls at everyone.

Whoosh! Thump!

One caught Izzy in the face. Angrily,
she chucked it back at Tennyson—but it
hit Jamal instead. Then the three of them
started throwing paper balls . . .

. . . right at Miss Cross as she walked back into the room.

"Pack that up!" she shouted. "Right. On the bench!"

It was a *bit* of a squeeze now.

Before long, they were joined by Stephanie and David—

"Bench!"

—Olive and Zidan—

"Bench!"

—and Lee-Yong.

"BENCH!"

"There is no room on the bench!" they said.
"Then *find* room!" Miss Cross told them.

And they had to. Higher . . .

. . . and higher . . .

. . . until the whole class was there!

Miss Cross
could hardly
believe her eyes.

"I've never seen anything like this!" she said,
shaking her head. "Now I have no class to teach!"
She sat down on one of the children's chairs . . .

. . . HARD.

"Oh, no," she groaned. "Nothing is going right this morning!" Then she noticed a dozen pairs of eyes staring at her. "All right," sighed Miss Cross. "I'll go on the bench, too."

And she did.
But not for long.
There was a *wibble.*

Then a *wobble.*

Then . . .

CRASH!

Luckily, nobody was hurt.

At that very moment, a ray of bright sunshine came through the large window. It shone on the children and their teacher like a heavenly light.

"Would you believe it?" smiled Miss Cross. "I think my headache is gone!"

The children looked at each other. Little grins began to appear on their faces. Then they all burst out laughing, joined by Miss Cross.

"We're sorry, Miss!" said the children together.
"It's all right," Miss Cross told them. "You really
are good children!"

The door opened, and the principal stuck his head in. "The trip to the zoo is back on!" he announced. "The bus driver has just turned up. Hurry up, get ready everyone!"

"Hurray!" shouted the children gleefully.

And they didn't
have to be told twice.